The Lisson Green Chronicles

LEON–SPIT ON THE MIC

The Lisson Green Chronicles

LEON-SPIT ON THE MIC

Ola Laniyan-Amoako
Lyrics by Jimi Vega Morales

Urbantopia collection

URBANTOPIA COLLECTION

Published by Urbantopia Books
121 Gloucester Place
London
W1J 6JU

www.urbantopia.co.uk

First published 2009 by Urbantopia Books

Printed in England by CPI Antony Rowe Ltd

For my little star... Ruben.
A big thank you to my number 1 fan...
Kemi – my big sister

CHAPTER 1

THE FAMILIAR sound of the estate whistle instantly broke me away from my favourite dream. I tried hard to fight it, tried to stay asleep and ignore the repetitive high-pitched coo coo bird imitation, but there was nothing I could do. I squeezed my eyes tight shut in the hope that the darkness would return and the chanting of my name, "Leman... Leman... Leman!" would continue, but instead the bright gleam from the summer sun invaded my sight.

The whistling continues as I sluggishly roll out of bed. I know who it is. It can only be Robert. He is the only person that would dare to disturb my summer holiday snooze. I look up at my microphone-shaped clock. "9.30!" I scream to myself. Is this brother crazy? 9.30 on a summer holiday morning! Only crazy Rob would be up. He'd be up at the crack of dawn, determined to practice shooting hoops. Determined to practice his three pointer shots.

Determined to perfect his game. Robert is a 15-year-old, 5'6" boy on a mission to be an international basketball player. He said he knew he was born to play and nothing was going to hold him back. Not his strict Nigerian mum, not some girl and most certainly, not some hater.

"I ain't getting caught up in no knife crime, become a statistic. Nah mate. I want bigger and better. You hearing me bruv?" he would say this on a daily basis with a smile across his face and the dream in his eyes. His ambition was wild and I ain't one to be grudging a guy, but why the hell did I have to suffer in his mission?

Slowly, I walk over to the large window and slide it to the left.

"Yo blod, you mad? D'you know what time it is?" I yell.

"Time to play ball man. It's late."

"Are you dizzy blod? It's 9.30."

"Leman man, come on. You know if we go courts later, the mans would have taken over the place and all them lot do is play ruffian b ball." He answers as he bounces his big orange ball hard against the concrete floor.

"Gimme an hour," I answer, shaking my head.

"An hour? You taking the Michael? Jeese man! An hour!" he exclaims, holding his ball close to his chest ready to bounce it against the wall.

"Mans need to freshen up. One hour."

He kisses his teeth and walks off. I kiss my teeth and slide the window back.

9.30 on a summer holiday morning. This was just not right. The law of teenagers states you didn't rise before 11.30. That's what Dad used to say whenever Mum tried to wake Latisha up. I glance at my reflection in the mirror. I can't find what I'm looking for so I step closer. I stare at myself with my nose right up against the mirror. Still no beard. Dad said his facial hair started growing when he was about fourteen. I'm fifteen and there's not even a sign of stubble. Mum says it was the white in him that made him so hairy.

All the boys at the youth club have facial hair and they get the girls because of it. Nadine Simmonds only seems to talk to the guys with facial hair.

I rub some of Latisha's hair cream across my chin: the bottle says some stuff about making hair grow quick, with any luck, it might just help me. It might help me grow that bad man goatee, the one that the men at the barbers shape up carefully with the clippers.

I take a step backwards and hold my toothbrush in position. The walls seem to push against space and time, widening it into a big arena just like the O2. I'm on stage and the crowd is going mad.

"Leman! Leman! Leman!" They chant as I shake my head and bounce from my knees. I feel the lyrics bubbling up in my stomach, rising slowly through my veins; like the hulk, I'm morphing from Leon to Leman: the master of the mic, the man whose skills bring out the chills. I can feel the notes moving in my blood, through my heart and out of my lungs. As I open my mouth to spit on the mic, the crowd goes crazy. Nadine Simmonds screams with excitement.

CHAPTER 2

I PUSH the button to call the lift. It makes a funny sound like an alien dying, but nothing happens. I push the silver square button again, hard. The lift groans and I hear the clanging noises of the chain pulling it up slowly. As the door opens, I walk into the dark dirty box. *Why can't people just use the toilet, why always the lift?* I wonder to myself as I cover my nose with one hand and reluctantly push the button inside the lift with the other hand. The lift moans loudly again and I'm convinced it's going to stop in between floors. I'm convinced I'm going to get stuck in this smelly box on a hot summer's morning at 10.30.

I'm so relieved when the flashing lights tell me I'm on the ground floor that I run out before the doors are fully open. I look around the grey concrete buildings. All the balconies are bare. No doubt the adults are at work and the normal kids are still in bed asleep.

I pull up my beltless jeans and bounce with my bad buoy swagger. From a distance I can hear the vibrating sound of the bouncing ball. Robert is practicing shooting his three pointers whilst Rianna is stood under the net like a loyal slave, catching the ball and throwing it back at him.

"Yo!" I call out as I walk into the high-fenced court.

"You're late mate. I've already recruited." Robert laughs as he runs towards the hoop and slam dunks the ball.

"Booyaow!" he yells whilst Rianna screams and rushes out of his way. She runs in my direction with her curly ponytail swishing from side to side.

"You alright Leon?" She asks giving me her Kodak smile and flashing her big, brown eyes.

"Yeah man. What's going on? Why you here so early? Where's Nadine?" I ask, looking around.

"Why you asking about Nadine? You fancy her?" She asks with her hands on her hips. My heart beats fast. Yes, I do fancy her, but I don't want Rianna knowing that, she'll turn it into some big embarrassing ordeal. That's what girls do; they make a big fuss about anything and everything.

"Nah man," I answer calmly. "Just wondering why you here alone init?"

She cocks her head to the side and stares at me – scanning me for the truth.

"Seen!" she finally replies. "She's coming feathers later. Robert knocked for me init so I just came down. I was already up."

"Oi!" Robert shouts as he releases the ball from his wrist straight into the netted hoop. "Let's play"

I walk over to him, stand opposite him. He bounces the ball to me, I bounce it back. He begins bouncing the ball, steps back and calculates his moves in his head. He bobs his head up and down like the ball. It is almost hypnotising. I squat low in defence mode and follow him around with my hands out. He moves left, I defend left. He moves right, I defend right, I blink, he steps left, bounces right, pushes me aside with his body and BAM! In the hoop goes the ball. *Dam he is good*. We swap round. He bounces the ball to me, I chest pass it back to him, he bounces it back again and I'm ready. I take quick sharp steps from the left to the right. I turn my side towards him and bounce hard. He comes at me defensively trying to block my every move. I move left, I shuffle backwards, forcing him to move back. He stretches out his hand and tries to get the ball but he can't. I hear his frustration. I spin round, stand in position ready to shoot. I flick my wrist and as the ball flies up in the air, he jumps up high and slaps it into the other direction. I swear in frustration whilst Rianna cheers loudly and laughs.

"Heavy!" she yells. "That was heavy."

CHAPTER 3

THE CLUB is packed out already. The badminton nets are up and some of the younger kids are attempting to hit the shuttlecock over the creamy-coloured net. Anne, the youth worker, is sat in the office behind her thick-rimmed glasses, chatting on the phone. Rianna rushes off and leaves us as we take our time chatting to Philip, the big black youth worker with the perfect moustache.

"Are you two coming to studio?" He asks.

"Yah man," responds Robert enthusiastically.

I definitely want to go to the studio but I hate it when there are too many people in there. It's stupid, but it makes me nervous. All their noise and laughter always makes me forget my lyrics.

"Leon? You on it?" Philip asks.

I nod my head and he looks happy.

As we make our way downstairs to the bottom hall, I can hear music booming up from the gym.

'Freeze' by T Pain is playing, which means Nadine, Celestine and Rianna are practising their routine. Those girls love dancing, especially Rianna; always body popping and bouncing. She's the best of the three, but Nadine is the prettiest. I walk over to the big balcony and look down into the open top gym.

They are all dressed in track suits and belly tops. Nadine is so choong. Her ponytails swish from side to side as she moves her head to the beat. I eye her up and down. Her fair skin reddens as she bursts out laughing when they mess up the move. Rianna doesn't laugh. She looks annoyed by their lack of seriousness.

I watch them for a while until Phil plugs in the PS3. The boys and I gravitate towards the television screen, fighting and arguing about who is going to go first. I stand back and laugh. Right now all I really feel like doing is practising my lyrics. I don't want to mess up in the studio.

"Hi Leon!" I hear from behind me. The dancing crew are walking towards me, smiling. I lean on a pillar, rub my chin and play with my imaginary facial hair. I try to look my coolest, my baddest.

"You alright ladies?" I slur, nodding my head. Celestine stops in front of me, smiling. I swear she fancies me.

"You not playing?" She asks, pointing to the television screen.

"Nah man. It's long. Too many people." I say

whilst desperately trying to think of what to say to include Nadine in the conversation. I just want her to talk to me. Take notice of me.

"You alright Nadine?" I finally muster up the courage to ask her as she holds an Evian bottle to her mouth. She nods as she swallows the water. I notice a drop roll down her arm and fall flat on her exposed belly. She is so foinnee.

"Hi Leon," she answers, uninterested, then turns to look at the TV screen.

"You guys dance bad. The routine is tight," I continue. She turns around, smiling, and I can see she is about to open her mouth when Celestine speaks.

"Oh, you were watching?" she asks playfully, slapping my arm lightly.

"Yeah... so where did you guys learn to dance?" I ask, trying to evoke some conversation from Nadine, but yet again Celestine jumps in.

"I learnt from my brother. He loved dancing and he used to perform in concerts and that." Celestine natters continuously and Nadine can't seem to get a word in edgeways.

"What 'bout you Nadine?" I ask when Celestine stops to take a breath.

"I've been going to Sylvia Young since I was about five. Mum made me do ballet. Rianna does ballet with me too," she answers shyly.

"You do ballet?" I asked, impressed.

"Yeah," she smiles.

"So, can you dance on your toes and that?" I ask, fascinated. She looks really happy I've asked her. She is just about to launch into giving me the details when Rianna's high-pitched voice turns her head.

"Oi! Girls! Break done man, we need to practice."

Nadine tuts and begins to walk off.

"Oi, Nadine!" I call out in attempt to quickly get more conversation out of her.

"Yeah?" she asks as she turns to face me.

"You have to show me that toes business later."

She laughs and walks off. I made Nadine Simmonds laugh. I'm a bad man. I made Nadine Simmonds laugh.

CHAPTER 4

"LADS, STUDIO in ten minutes," Philip announces in his deep baritone. My heart begins to beat hard against my rib cage. I'm excited yet I'm scared. I know studio is going to be jam-packed with all the boys. I know they are going to be looking for a way to take the mickey out of anyone who gives them the opportunity. I also know it's going to be a wild competition to see who can get on the mic first. I love studio. I love being in the studio, hearing myself chat on the playback, but man I hate the crowd eagerly watching and preying for jokes.

I stand against the wall, silently rehearsing my lines in my head. Over and over I repeat my new lyrics and, in my head, it sounds wicked.

Slowly the small dimly lit studio becomes packed out with eight hormonal teenagers bouncing wildly with excitement, dying to show off their talents. Tall, dark Mensah stands in front of the mic before anyone has a chance to say a word and he begins chatting. Most of his lines are muffled and it is difficult to work out if he is trying to rap or chat. His talentless display instils some confidence in me as I know I'm way better than that.

"Switch!" Yells Philip, who is clearly unimpressed by Mensah's exhibition.

Vanilla steps up to the mic and a cloud of confidence surrounds him like he is already world-famous. He bounces from his knees, bobs his head hard and counts the beats carefully before dropping his lyrics. He flows like a kite moving in the wind. Each sentence links to the next without hesitation or complication. Each line rhymes poetically with the next.

For a short, blonde, blue-eyed boy, his lines are bad. He gets us all excited and, although I'm green with envy, even I have to salute him with our legendary 'blap, blap, blap'. He smiles his small cheeky grin and pulls his white cap far down so we can barely see his eyes. Philip stops him, then begins formulating a beat.

"OK, run that one more time. Listen to the beat, yeah. Take your time and breathe Paul," says Philip.

"Vanilla! Phil. Vanilla!"

"Yes, Vanilla," Phil laughs.

The beat is fast-paced and easy to rhyme with; well at least it seems so as Vanilla rides it with ease.

He spits on the mic and throws his words with feeling and passion whilst the rest of us stand entranced by one of the few white boys on the estate.

"Nice, nice. You smashed it bruv," says Philip. "Who is next?"

Everyone is now prang. No one wants to go after Vanilla. Who the hell wants to chat after someone has just dropped a master piece?

"Skull Head, go chat man," Mensah says, volunteering the youngest and craziest boy in the studio. Skull Head, otherwise known as James, is only 13 but he is one crazy kid. He is volatile with a very short temper. He is always getting caught up in some sort of brawl. When he is happy, he is cool, but man, the boy can switch on you one time.

Skull Head looks surprisingly nervous as he stops in front of the mic. We all watch eagerly awaiting what he has to show us.

"Yo! Phil, I want to start off different yeah?" he says pulling up his baggy, beltless jeans.

"The mic's yours big man," answers Philip as he relaxes in his big leather chair.

Skull Head shuts his eyes tight and opens up his mouth wide like he is about to scream, but instead he begins to sing. He sings like he's been going to church every Sunday since he was five. His voice is soulful and we are mesmerised as he sings about a girl in year nine.

'I...think you are soooooooooo pretty girl. Girl in class T, year nine, you are something so fine. Yeahhhhhhh.'

Suddenly, out of the blue, he switches into a fast-paced rap.

"Blap! Blap! Blap!" we all jump up excitedly because the originality is just too much.

For a while he switches from song to rap and when Phil applies a beat to his work, they blend like snow and ice.

I'm eager yet fearful about picking up the mic. I know my work is tight. I'm a lyrical poet and I know it, but today I see my competition and it evokes fear into my bloodstream.

"Leman! Step man," Philip yells from the booth. My hands shake lightly so I quickly make a fist. I clench my fist tight and step closer to the mic. I bob my head while I try to hype myself up by picturing a packed out arena.

As my mouth opens up so does my fist. I express myself both verbally and physically, illustrating constructively with my hand and fingers. I see the boys bounce their head to my flow and I ride the beat like a wave. Carefree, I bounce. Comfortably, I chat. Confidently, I spit on the mic and they are feeling me. I'm smiling. I'm laughing. Adrenaline is pumping through me especially when the boys salute me.

"Hip-hop, garage, you choose,
but you lose,
I had the game in checkmate
in 2 moves,
a top badman, fs a 2,2s,
I'm hard wid a pen, firing like ripped barz from the feds,
I can take you out now plus half of the endz.

Yessir, that's me,
The man with the magical tongue,
The lyrical G.

They call me the man with the...."

Nadine Simmonds walks in mid-flow and I forget my next line. She stands there watching me watching her with my tongue hanging out silently over the mic.

CHAPTER 5

"WHAT'S WRONG with you? Why's your faced shaped like a baboon's bottom?" Latisha bursts into floods of laughter over her own joke. I stick two fingers up at her.

"Not in my house," Dad growls from behind his newspaper. I swear his papers are transparent. How he manages to see everything going on whilst reading his Daily Mirror amazes me.

Latisha and I help Mum set the table while Dad sits reading his paper. I reminisce about today's embarrassing display in front of Nadine Simmonds. She walked into the room and I got so nervous, I froze. My lyrics dried up from my mind's eye, my crowd faded and I became beardless Leon just like that. The boys thought it was hilarious. They cackled with wicked laughter and mimicked me all the way home.

Robert was the worst; he crossed his eyes and left his tongue hanging silently. The boys laughed and laughed. I felt close to tears, but I held it back. I clenched my fist and simply said "Whateva man!" I said it like I didn't care, but I did. I cared that the boys saw me mess up on the mic, but, most importantly, I cared that I'd humiliated myself in front of Nadine. My stomach churned and rumbled and although the smell of my mother's curry goat danced sweetly on the hairs of my nostrils, I didn't feel hungry. I looked down at my plate and all I could see was a picture of me on the mic, goggle-eyed and tongue-tied. I poke at the rice and push the peas around the plate. I chew at length on a piece of meat.

"Don't stop man, that sounded heavy from outside," she had said, while standing in the doorway. I should have carried on. I should have had the confidence to go on. Jigger man would never have stopped because Beyonce walked into the room and nor would Kanye. I can't even begin to imagine Dizzie Rascal getting tongue-tied. He's a lyrical don and so am I, so I should have been able to go on.

I drop my fork on my plate and the clattering sound draws everyone's head up in my direction.

"Leon! What's wrong with you boy?" Mum asks irritated. If there is one thing my mum can't stand, it's wasting food. She would rather make you eat up your food and watch you throw it back up again than allow you to chuck it in the bin.

"I'm not hungry, can I leave the table?" I ask. Latisha stares straight at me from her seat then looks at Mum then at Dad. She knows what is coming next. I know what is coming next but right now I just want to go to my room and have some think time. My mother sucks her teeth hard like a market woman from Jamaica. My father places his knife and fork carefully on his plate. He interlocks his fingers and rests his chin on the bridge he has built with his hands. His nostrils flare. My mother takes a deep breath in.

"Leon? Is there a problem?" Dad asks as he finishes chewing.

"Don't get me angry Leon. You know the rules of the table," Mum adds.

"What's wrong?" Dad asks again, calmly.

"I don't care what's wrong," interrupts Mum. "Number one, you'd better finish your food. I didn't slave away at work to have you waste food. Number two. Dinner time is family time. No one leaves the table. Do you know how privileged you are? Some people don't have food and some people don't have families to share meal times with. Furthermore, how many children on this estate do you know have a live in father? Meal times are family times and we stay at the table till we have all finished."

My mother heaves and Latisha stares at me with a wide smirk across her face. She is enjoying this drama: she loves it when I get into trouble.

"Leon," Dad calls out in a controlled tone. I look up at him and stare at his well-trimmed facial hair. Thin down the sides, carefully cut beneath his nose, around his jaw and well constructed at his chin. I can see his jaw moving but I don't hear a sound. I'm too busy studying his face.

"Leon!" my mother shrieks. Latisha bursts out laughing and pointing at me. "Did you not hear your dad?" she yells.

I look at Latisha. She is still in stitches and I swear I'm going to jump up and kill her with my bare hands.

"You may leave the table," my father states. My mother huffs and puffs, and Latisha looks shocked.

"Leanne, calm down. Leave the boy. He looks troubled. Woman you love to moan too much." I hear my father say as I push my chair in and run down the stairs straight into my room.

CHAPTER 6

I LIE on my bed with my stereo playing Dizzie's new album. I play it low 'cause I know mum is already annoyed with me. An hour passes and I play Jay-Z's new blueprint album. I listen intently trying to get some inspiration, but nothing comes to me. A gentle knock on the door startles me. I know it can only be Latisha. I know she is coming to fill me in on my post-exit dining table drama. I know she's probably coming to cuss me for causing yet another argument between Mum and Dad.

"What?" I yell. I'm shocked when Dad's face appears around the door. I sit up as he walks towards me. He sits down next to me and takes a deep breath in.

"Leon," he says in his gentle yet deep tone.

"Yeah Dad," I answer, half frightened he is going to tell me off.

"What's going on?" he asks. "Leon, come on man,

tell me. I'm your dad. You can tell me anything. I know you well enough to know something's up. You're my favourite son," he laughs.

"I'm your only son," I smirk.

"And if you weren't, you'd still be my favourite, you know why? You know why?" he repeats in his young London-boy tone.

"Why dad?" I sigh, half interested in his theory.

"'Cause you look like me son. Not as handsome but look, look at our reflection. It's like they photocopied me. You're lucky son. You're lucky; you're a good-looking boy. You're going to get all the ladies." He laughs and throws his arms around my neck. I laugh because that is a great thought.

"Did loads of girls fancy you?" I ask as we both stare at our reflection. We chuckle and we can see we have the same dimples on our left cheeks as we laugh.

"Girls? Yeah, they loved me. They used to call me Leeeeeeeeroy, the finnnnnnneee boy." I laugh.

"Is that what it is? A girl?" he asked with his serious face.

My dad is a handsome man. Fair skin, high cheek bones, smooth skin. He is crisp and clean with his hair cut to perfection. Like mum said, not many children on the estate have a live-in dad. I'm the envy of most of my friends. Robert says it's the white in him that makes him a family man. He says if my dad was a proper black man, he would have left like most of the other fathers on the estate but I know he is just jealous. He is jealous 'cause his dad lives in Nigeria and he rarely gets to see him.

"Who is she?" he asks.

I shrug.

"Is it the Rianna girl, Angie's daughter?"

I shake my head viciously. "Nah man, Rianna's just a friend."

"So it is a girl? Who is it?"

My mother bursts into the bedroom before I have a chance to answer.

"What's this? Boys' meeting? Leon you better...."

"Leanne, leave him man. Can't you see we're chatting?" My dad interrupts her.

"Chatting 'bout what?" she yells in annoyance.

"Woman! Please! Leave man. This is man to man chat."

"But..." she insists.

"Go! Leanne, he'll be down to finish his food in a minute man. Relax."

My mother turns around, annoyed.

"Sweet heart" my father calls out after her in his charming voice. She stops and turns her head.

"I'm sorry. Look two minutes yeah. We'll be up." My mother melts and smiles. She always does when he refers to her as *sweetheart*. It's like her melt button.

"So go on son. Tell me."

"Nadine Simmonds, she's in my year in school."

"Is she pretty?" he asks eagerly.

"What?" I screech in excitement. "She is foiinee... serious gash Dad. I really like her. The way she smiles..." I stare into thin air as I remember her face.

"Rahtid," Dad laughs.

"She's perfect."

"So, what happened? You asked her out?"

I throw my head back and raise my eyebrow. How can I ask her out? She is out of my league.

"She's out of my league," I reply, deflated from my high.

"What!" he screams. "League? Hey boy, no girl is out of your league. Are you listening? What is it? Because she is pretty?"

I nod.

"Look at yourself in the mirror. Son you are fine. Once you believe that, she will too."

"She only talks to the older guys."

"'Cause they are the only ones brave enough to step up to her. Look son, just be yourself. You are a funny guy. Make her laugh and she'll be putty in your hands."

"I messed up today Dad. Totally embarrassed

myself in front of her. I was on the mic chatting, flowing and when she walked in, I froze. I forgot my lines. I nearly died. I felt so embarrassed, I can't face her again." I confess with my head hung down.

With his arm around me, Dad grabs my shoulder tight.

"You messed up? No biggie. If you can learn to laugh about it then it will be forgotten. The boys will tease you, the girls might, but I swear, if you laugh about it then everyone will move on. Believe me."

"You think so?" I ask, staring at him

"I know so. Trust me. Look Lee, jokes aside. You are 15; I don't want you to focus on girls too much yeah? Read your books, have your hobby but don't get too involved with girls yet. Nadine Simmonds? Have your careful fun, but not too much. Stay focused on your future. Your mum and I didn't focus and it stumped us. We started a family young and I want you to enjoy life first. Yeah? You hearing me?" He says, his face serious and without a smile.

"Yes Dad." I answer.

"Promise?"

"Promise" I mutter.

"Come on, you best go eat before your mum kills us both." We both stand up. He pats me on the back before we both hug.

"Thanks Dad" I whisper.

"It's cool. Remember, laugh at yourself and make her smile."

CHAPTER 7

MY ALARM bleeps at 9.00am. I rise out of bed with a spring in my toes and a bounce in my knees. I'm up early because today I'm on it. I'm perfecting my game. I'm writing my lyrics, I'm practising my flow; I'm jumping to the pace. I'm a bad man and I know it. A lyrical poet, a lyrical gangster, a lyrical genius, a lyrical mastermind and the whole world is going to know it. My thoughts are instantly broken by Latisha's screeching voice.

"Leon!" she yells before sticking her head into my room.

"Have you seen my chocolate-coloured skinny jeans and my black baggy top, the one with the magic beans thing on it?"

I kiss my teeth and answer in rhyme.

"Baggy shirt, skinny jeans?,
Wont catch ME wearin' that bruv, not by any means....
Chocolate fudge, yeah, I like that! But magic beans?,

Oi,.... they only exist in cinema screens!,
But I have heard beans got lots of protein?, start eatin tish, you never know
You might grow big and strong like Wolverine,
Then maybe, you'll grow out of them skinny jeans!"

Latisha kisses her teeth long and hard before she finally leaves my room.

At 11 o'clock I'm rehearsed out. I have a shower and rub some of Latisha's cream across my chin. I gaze at myself in the mirror.

"Leeeeon, the fine buoy," I chuckle as Dad's words ring in my ears over and over. *If you believe it, she will too.*

At 11.30, I'm surprised Robert hasn't knocked for me. I leave the flat and make my way towards Robert's flat. There is no way he is still sleeping. Outside his red door, I can hear his little brothers running round making noise. I ring the door bell and the 11-year-old demon twins open the door.

"Hello," says Ramon.

"Hello," echoes Raphael.

"Is Robert in?" I ask.

They shrug the way they always do when you ask them a question.

"Is Robert in?" says Ramon.

"Dunno Ray, is he?" answers Raphael.

"Guys stop fooling around, is Rob in?" I ask again

with a strong desire to grab their necks and knock their heads together.

"He might be, but I believe he has company," says Ramon.

"Company." echoes Raphael.

I kiss my teeth and push past them. I walk past the messy kitchen down to the first landing. I peek into the front room. Cushions are sprawled on the floor. Empty food bowls are on the centre table and the television is on full blast playing 'You the best' by Drake.

I knock on Robert's bedroom door, to which he yells "Go away!"

"It's me man!" I call back.

The door opens and he steps out and shuts the door as though he is hiding something.

"Yo! What's going on?" I ask him.

"Nuffink man!" he responds instantly.

"You indoors at this time, not on road, not on the court. Warrior?" I laugh, but he doesn't.

"Nah man I..." A crashing noise in the kitchen interrupts him. "Oi you two," he yells as he runs up the stairs towards the demon twins. I laugh whilst opening his bedroom door.

"Nah don't!" he yells, looking back at me, but it's too late. I walk into his room and Rianna is in his bed. Her eyes are wet and a deep shade of red. She sniffs and quickly sits up.

"It's not what you fink yeah?" she cries out loudly before I have a chance to speak.

"Don't go chatting to people yeah? It ain't what it looks like," she continues to cry whilst she gets out of his bed fully dressed ready to put on her shoes. Robert rushes back into his room. I give him the look and he shakes his head dismissively. He walks towards Rianna who is stamping her foot into her trainers.

"Ri Ri, sit down B," he says to her with great concern in his eyes. "Look Lee is going yeah, it's cool, just sit down. Where you going to go?" He pushes her back down to sit on the bed. She bursts into loud cries and I'm scared.

"What's going on?" I ask

"Not now man. Look, I'm coming club later yeah. I'll catch you later. Lee man please."

I look at Rianna. I've never seen her like this; she's like a proper tomboy. Always acts like one of the lads. Never cries about anything and I can't even begin to think why she would be in such a state at Robert's house. Either way, I leave his room quietly.

"Leon," Robert calls out.

"Yeah?"

"Don't tell anyone she's here yeah?"

I nod and walk out of the door.

Chapter 8

I WALK into the youth club anxious of who might make fun of me.

"Yo Leon, your lyrics were tight yesterday" Mensah says slapping my arm in greeting.

I'm waiting for him to turn the compliment into a joke.

"Yeah thanks man," I answer.

"You rocked that beat boy," he continues enthusiastically, bouncing like he can hear me flowing in his head.

"Yeah, till I froze..." I laugh pretentiously. "I was all tongue-tied, that was mad funny," I continue.

"Yeah man! Eh, don't be freezing out at the talentville spit competition next week," he chuckles.

"The what?" I ask, confused.

"That website, talentville has organised the spit on the mic competition man. Next week at Moberly. You have to enter man."

The thought of it excites me but I'm also frightened; a competition where crowds get to hear you spit on the mic!

"Hey Philip," Mensah yells whilst using his long arms to beckon Philip over.

"Yo Philip, tell my man bout the spit on the mic competition. He has to be in the crew man." Mensah pleads. Philip shakes his head.

"Team's full man. Only six allowed in a group and he weren't here the other morning to put his name down. Sorry bruv, next time," Philip answers before patting my back and walking off.

"That's dark man. Sorry yeah..." Mensah concludes.

"It's cool man. They ain't ready for me," I laugh and walk off.

As I make my way down the stairs, I hear laughter. I know it's Nadine. She is stood against the wall in the stairway talking to Jermaine. Jermaine the sixth former. Jermaine the big man with enough facial hair to be mistaken for a monkey. I walk past them avoiding eye contact.

"Hi Leon," she calls as I continue down the steps.

"You alright Nadine?" I answer whilst turning my head round. She smiles her perfect white teeth smile and I continue down the steps. I walk past the studio and notice the lights are on. I walk in to find Philip playing with the beats. He looks up.

"Big man!" he yells out, smiling.

"Can I?" I ask, heading for the mic.

"Yessir!" he answers.

I'm in heaven. In the studio alone without some crazy, critical audience. Undiluted time with the silver lady and foam afro. The microphone.

I start my rhyming or as Mum calls it, 'my poem'. I bounce, hold on to my skull and shut my eyes as I lay down my masterpiece.

I'm on my own ting,
live life like my own king,
flow hard, like a bee sting
,live life in full swing,
But let me tell you bruv
bout one ting...

I'm riding the wave; I'm flying high like a kite. I'm in a new world, in another dimension. I'm Leman with the magical tongue and if you don't know, you better get to know.

I shut my eyes and recite my lines, bouncing back and forth and smiling hard.

I come to an end and open my eyes to see Nadine next to me. She takes the mic and sings the last few words from my piece. She sounds heavy.

"Blap, blap, blap" Philip yells.

"I didn't know you could sing," I say to Nadine who is stood with a massive smile across her face.

"Yeah, I sing," she answers.

"But don't try test me," I laugh. "The heat from my flow will hurt you four show."

"Says the man whose words once froze," she laughs back.

"Well that's what pretty girls do to a man, you get me. Get you all tongue-tied and ish."

She blushes and her cheeks turn a shade of candyfloss pink.

"What you blushing for. I ain't talking about you." I tease. She laughs and slaps my arm.

"Neva said you was... Oi, have you seen Rianna today?"

"Nah," I lie.

"I called her all morning. Bet the lazy thing is still sleeping."

"Yeah," I reply, not wanting to get twisted in the big lie.

"Where's Robert?" she asks.

"With the evil twins."

She laughs. "You so stupid. Evil twins you know. You are too funny."

Hear that? I'm *too* funny.

CHAPTER 9

"WHY WAS Rianna at your house the other day?"

"She lives downstairs; she's always at my house," Robert answers in a matter of fact way, evading my real question.

"Why was she crying?"

I bounce the ball away from his reach and he falls into the defence position, blocking my every move.

"Ask her man. I can't be chatting her business," he answers impatiently as I pass him and do a lay up towards the basket.

"Just tell me man. Are you going out with Rianna bruv?" I laugh as my ball goes through the hoop.

"Nah man!" he yells as he retrieves the ball. "Look! I didn't do anything to make her cry man. Talk to her. Read her story, whatever, just change the subject man and let me concentrate. Mans have a big game coming up."

We practice for a while, talking about school and what we are going to do when we leave.

"I'm off to the States," Robert yells as he swings on the ring.

"Like your mum would let you go," I laugh.

"Yo bruv, once I'm 18, I'm free from her strict ways man. My sister says 'Rob, just pass your GCSEs and that will keep her off your back' so that's what I'm going to do. Play ball, pass my exams and get the hell out of here."

"Seen!" I answer breathlessly.

"Yo bruv, I'm a warrior. I'll fight till I get to where I'm going."

I laugh and stop. I'm tired. Unlike Robert, I'm human and I get tired and fed up of shooting hoops.

"Yo Leman, you like Nadine?" He asks sitting down next to me on the bench.

"She's alright," I answer nonchalantly.

"Whatever man, you froze when she walked into the studio."

"Bygones man. Yeah I froze and what?" I answer defensively.

"You like her init. Just say it," he asks again as he cradles the big orange ball in his arms.

"Yeah... I like her," I finally answer.

"You going to ask her out?"

I shrug. I want her to be my girlfriend but I don't

want to ask her out. What if she says 'No'? That would be so embarrassing.

"I bet you won't. Bet you £5, you won't ask her out," Robert says, jumping off his seat and bouncing his orange baby.

"Don't watch me man. Just have your money ready," I answer cockily.

"When?"

"At the big game."

"Tonight?"

"Yeah, if she's there."

"Off course she's there. Them lot are dancing at the game."

"Is it? Seen. Anyway check these lines man. Tell me what you think," I say quickly in order to change the subject.

He holds the ball against his chest and I shut my eyes as usual then I begin to flow. I ride the airways and begin to bounce. I'm controlling my breathing as I chat 'cause that's what I've seen Kanye doing. I'm twisting some lines and expanding some words as Dizzie Rascal does. Mensah and Vanilla walk into the court, I don't stop. Instead I insert a line, laughing at myself.

"Yeah it's me, the man that froze at the sight of beauty. What can I say, the girl was a cutie? She was the one with the big mamma bootie."

They all bend over laughing before they salute me and Vanilla takes over from my last word.

In a circle we stand, bouncing and bobbing, playing with lines. Messing with lyrics and forgetting the time. Getting excited and saluting at each other. Good times.

CHAPTER 10

"WHAT TIME you leaving for the game?" Latisha asks as I rhyme to myself and brush my low-trimmed hair.

"Oi!" she yells out, frustrated at being ignored, her ultra-fair skins begins doing the traffic light routine. From light brown, to pink and slowly to red.

"Why?" I ask her, still facing the mirror.

"I'll walk down with you init."

"I might not want you to walk down with me," I smile before barging past her.

"Look Dark Vader, you don't have to worry, I won't wreck your game. It's just... I don't want to go alone."

"Not my fault you're a Billy no mates," I smirk as she follows me to my room.

"Marcia is going but I'm meeting her there. Look, what time you leaving?"

"You scared to walk alone?" I tease with my back to her.

"No!" she yells, kissing her teeth, then she continues to rant. "Look Lee, I haven't got all day to have this pointless conversation with you. I'm not scared to walk alone, I just don't want to. If we are going to the same game, we might as well go together. LEON!"

"Alright! Alright Lati, I'm leaving at 6.30 on the dot. No long tings. I ain't running on BMT, I'm running on GMT. You get me?" I answer calmly as I slap on some aftershave.

"Why couldn't you just say that to start with dark man?"

"Because I love winding you up pink lady," I laugh.

"What have I told you about referring to each other by the colour of your skin?" Mum yells.

"Pink lady? Dark man? I want none of that type of language in my house. It's derogatory. Black people went through a lot to stop people calling them names and..."

My mum, the teaching assistant, begins to lecture us on the history of black Britain. Latisha huffs, I puff, but neither of us dares to interrupt her.

"Are you hearing me?" she asks firmly.

"Yes Mum," we both sing in chorus.

"What time are you going to the game?"

"We're leaving at 6.30," I answer.

"Be back by 10.30," she states.

"Mum!" Latisha moans.

"10.30 or I'll come over and get you myself. Don't try me," Mum replies and continues to mumble as she turns her back to us and walks up the stairs.

"Lati, one hour yeah and I'm missing like the money after a bank robbery. Be ready."

My sixteen year old, fair skin sister walks off into her room as her mobile begins to ring. With only one year between us, Latisha and I have always been close.

Although we share the same features such as our high cheekbones, thin lips and small eyes, our complexions differ drastically. Whilst I'm chocolate brown, she almost looks like caramel. Our relatives always used to make jokes about us and whether we were really siblings and Mum would get really irritated and yell. The concept of focusing on the colour of our skin annoys Mum. She said she had no doubt that one day Latisha would become self-conscious about her ultra light skin. What Mum fails to realise is that Latisha is far too vain to be self-conscious about her colour. She is too busy worrying about her model looks.

CHAPTER 11

MENSAH, VANILLA, Skull Head, Kiaron, Justine and Amelia are stood in a huddle outside Moberly sports centre. I stop close by them and listen to them practising their lines.

"What you guys doing?" I ask stupidly as though it isn't obvious.

"Rehearsing init?" Vanilla answers as he bounces up and down to Kiaron's flow.

"What for?" I continue.

"We're opening up the game bruv," Mensah states proudly.

"Don't lie," I answer shocked. I'm annoyed and jealous. I would have loved to open up the game. Can you imagine that? Me, flowing, spitting my rhymes and the crowd going crazy. This would have been a wicked time to get exposure. Give everyone around here a taste of my talent. See me do what I was born to do. But yet again, I seem to have missed the boat.

"See how you mans are. You couldn't even tell mans," I moan.

"Nah it ain't like that," Mensah insists. "Philip said to use it as an opportunity to practice for the spit on the mic."

"Seen. You guys proper like to keep mans in the dark. Spit on the mic man. How come I weren't told about that man?"

The huddle breaks up and we all begin to walk towards the indoor court.

"Philip asked us last Wednesday morning. He had to put the names through that day and you weren't there. He told us if we commit to it we would have to come in every morning to practice," Amelia states.

"Seen," I reply, sulking because I know exactly where I was last Wednesday morning. I was out on the court helping Robert practice.

Grumpily, I find myself a seat in the stalls and prepare to watch the game. The indoor court fills up slowly and the noise of loud chatter increases. I look around and see Latisha with Marcia chatting away. Rianna is sat with Celestine and Nadine. They are all coordinated in their baggy black combat trousers and black belly tops. Feels like everyone but me is performing tonight. I notice the evil twins and

Robert's older, pretty sister. To my shock they are sat down with Robert's mum. Robert's mum never comes to his games.

As the crew hype themselves up, the jealousy in my stomach breeds and multiplies. I wish I was performing. It's just so unfair.

"Oi, Leman, do you want to go on instead of me?" Mensah asks as he nervously moves his cap back and forth.

Suddenly the thought of me going on stage in front of all these people seems daunting. My heart wants to rip off his arm and say 'yes!' 'Yes off course! I'll go on bredwin. Have you heard my lyrics? Are they ready for me? Nah they ain't ready for me.' But my heart starts beating fast. My palms suddenly start clamming up and beads of sweat begin to form on my forehead.

"Nah man, you go," I answer shaking my head.

"Are you sure blod?" he asks me one more time and suddenly the hands on the clock freeze. Silence falls and everyone around me freezes. My heart thunders mercilessly and two small figures appear on either side of my shoulders.

"Leon, take the opportunity, it will let you shine. Say yes. Just do it. The girls will be screaming Leeeeeman, Leeeeman. Look at Nadine. She'll be so impressed," says the little figure on my right shoulder and, for moment, I get excited, I feel hyped. 'I'm a bad man' I think to myself, 'I'm going to mash up this place' but then the little figure on my left shoulder begins to speak.

"Are you mad? Are you crazy? Are you dizzie blod? You haven't practiced. You haven't worked with the rest of the group. What if you mess up in front of all these people? Especially Nadine. No way man, no way."

The hands on the clock begin to tick. The noise falls around me and people begin to move again.

"Nah man. Nah," I answer and as he turns his back to me I feel a great sense of regret.

The crew walk off into the middle of the court with two mics in hand. Philip drops the beat with a heavy bass line and one after the other they rhyme. When Vanilla comes on, the boys in the crowd go wild, whilst the girls clap hysterically. He overpowers the crowd and controls them as he drops his lyrics like a true professional. He hands the mic to Skull Head and when he breaks into song, the crowd is silent. They are mesmerised by his sweet boy voice. The crowd stand up to applaud them before they walk off the court. I should have said yes.

CHAPTER 12

ROBERT STARTS the game as always. Taller than the average fifteen-year-old, he has the advantage. The sound of the crowd alongside the squeaking of trainers against the polished floorboards is deafening. The game is fast and furious with the ball going from one end to the other in seconds. They score, we score, they score, we score. And as exciting as the game is, I'm unable to really enjoy it 'cause I'm kicking myself. I'm cursing myself out for being such a big baby. Mensah offered me the opportunity of a lifetime and I said 'No'. Today could have been my making yet my fear got the better of me. What kind of MC am I going to be?

I sit watching as 'the crew' discuss and dissect their performance over and over again. I just wish they would shut the hell up.

Robert slam dunks the ball into the net. He hangs

off the hoop and the crowd go wild, roaring with applause and laughter. The half-time whistle goes. We are ten points ahead.

The three girls position themselves on the court. Tight black vest, knee length tracksuits and knee pads with bright-red Adidas trainers. The beat from speakers pumps hard and they begin their well-coordinated movements. None of them miss a beat. Like well-tuned robots they dance in sync. Body popping and spinning on their knees. They look bad and the crowd shows its appreciation by clapping and whistling.

The atmosphere is hyped at half-time. The music plays loud. People are talking excitedly about the best shots and predicting scores for the second half. Others talk of the performances and come over to spud the group. The nonstop praises sicken me to the pit of my stomach so I decide to go out for some fresh air.

Outside, Nadine is stood alone with a bottle of water in her hand. I walk with a swagger and a lean up to her. Make myself look as cool as possible.

"Hey Nadine, you guys were heavy up in there."

"Thanks," she smiles shyly.

"Why you out here alone?" I ask as I get closer to her.

"Needed some fresh air. Plus Rianna is in one of her moods. Says we mashed up some of the steps."

"Nah man. You guys were off the hook. Making me want to learn how to dance."

She burst into laughter and her pretty eyes shut whilst her dimples appear.

"You still have to show me them ballet moves," I continue.

"You joker," she replies, slapping my arm. "So why you out here?" she asks.

"Come to talk to you init. Protect you from any crazy, wandering strangers," I laugh.

"Who told you I needed protection?" she smiles.

"You're a girl. All girls need protecting."

"Who told you that?" She yells.

"My dad," I answer, feeling confidently brave and cocky.

"Your dad? Sounds like my dad," she answers, staring me straight in the eyes.

"So do you have someone protecting you now?" I ask.

"What do you mean?" she says, leaning her head to the left.

"You know. Do you have a boyfriend and that?" I ask whilst the beating of my heart gets faster and harder.

"Boyfriend? Nah," she states.

"Seen. So... can I protect you 'cause I'd like to have your back and ish."

"What do you mean?" she asks.

The whistle sounds in the background, signalling the end of half-time. I hear the ball bouncing back and forth. The rubber soles squeaking on the floorboards and the roaring crowd.

"I mean, like can I be your boyfriend? Would you be my girl?"

She smiles from ear to ear and she looks so pretty. She runs her hand over her head and releases her ponytail. Her hair falls around her face and she looks amazing.

"No, you can't," she says, still grinning and shaking her head.

"OK," I answer, trying to keep my cool.

"We better go back in or we'll miss the game," she says as she heads in the direction of the indoor court.

CHAPTER 13

"YO BRUV, what happened to you yesterday man. You missed the end of the game and buoy, was it heavy? Yessir, it was bad! I stole the ball yeah, dribbled, and did a bad man lay up and bam! Hell the crowd went crazy. Them suckers...."

Robert continues to ramble on about yesterday but I'm only half listening.

Yesterday, I couldn't bear to go back inside after Nadine said 'no'. I felt so embarrassed and ashamed. I asked a girl out and she said no. When she initially said no, I thought she was joking 'cause of the way she was smiling. I wanted to cry and when I got home, I did. I buried my face into my pillow and cried. Nadine Simmonds had said a big fat no. How was I ever going to live that down? How was I going to tell Robert and how much fun was he going to make of me?

"Yo bruv, you listening? Yo, what's wrong with

you man? Face like thunder," Robert asks.

"Nuffink man," I answer.

"What man? What happened?" he asks in his concerned tone.

"I asked Nadine out yesterday and she said no."

Roberts's jaw drops.

"Don't lie?" he gasps.

I nod silently.

"Sorry man," he says and I'm shocked. I would have thought this was a perfect opportunity for him to make fun of me, but he doesn't, he just sits next to me in silence.

"Hey, guess what?" he says, breaking the depressing silence.

"What?" I answer solemnly.

"Celestine's on you," he laughs.

"Whatever man."

"Nah serious. Rianna says she's always going on about you. Leon this and Leon that. You should tap that," he says enthusiastically.

"Nah man... Celestine? Nah. Why does Rianna tell you everything? You guys are proper close init? Is there something you want to tell me bruv?"

He kisses his teeth and looks out of his bedroom window.

"Nah, Rianna my bredwin man. She lives

downstairs and she hates her dad so whenever he's home she always comes up to mine init."

"Seen. But would you thou? Would you go there?"

"Nah man. Rianna is too cool for that man. She's one of my boys. Come man, let's go court." He says reaching up onto his shelf for his big orange ball.

"Nah mate. I'm going studio. Practice with them lot."

"Yeah, they were bad last night init. The way Vanilla dropped it and Amelia followed through. It was rough, shame about Mensah though. He is tone deaf. That brother should stick to running."

"Don't be dark man. Mensah tries. He was proper boomy yesterday, he asked if I wanted to go instead of him."

"And what? You said no?" Robert gasps.

"Too short notice man," I answer.

"Are you dizzy blod? You ain't ever heard the phase, grab any opportunity with both hands. You said no? Yo bruv, that was real exposure time right there. You're a bad man and I know it so you need to let the whole world know it too man. You said no? Crazy fool!" he laughs, leaving me feeling even worse. I feel gutted I let that kind of opportunity slip by, so from now on, I'm going to make sure I'm always prepared. I'm going to make sure I take every given opportunity to practice. I ain't ever saying no again.

CHAPTER 14

I WALK into the club and it is quite empty. The group are huddled on the middle floor ready to practice whilst Rianna, Celestine and Nadine are on the lower level practicing. I avoid eye contact with Nadine as I walk past the gym straight into the studio.

In the small, dark, warm room. Philip is sat there making beats. As I walk in, he waves his big palms at me.

"Yes! Big man, rhyme to this for me yeah?"

I pick up the headphones and I feel my transformation. I don't care who is watching, I don't care who is listening. I've got no time for embarrassment, no space for failure. I listen to the beat for the first ten seconds. Rearrange my lyrics in my mind then drop it like it's hot. My eyes are shut, my vision is clear. The enormous stage in the big arena, the screaming fans. I chat about Nadine and what I want to do to her. How I want to protect her, kiss and caress her, and even I can't help thinking I'm a slick ass fool.

Let me tell you a story about this girl from the ends,
this girl's my special friend, someone who I can depend.
It's kinda funny though, she'll never know,
every time I see her, my heart's like Whoa!
Heaven knows, I'm only 15 years old!
And still, I can feel this crazy hold,
as strong as an iron mould,
somethin' like a common cold...
I don't think she's aware how much she holds,
as my pen hits the paper, my heart unfolds...
her beauty makes my heart deepen,
my heart weaken and,
yet this chick is not really seekin'
the kind of love that I want to give.

I open up my eyes to see the crew in the studio alongside the three girls.

"Wicked man! Yo, you need to upload that onto talentville. Log-on tonight to talentville.co.uk. Upload one minute of skill and get your friends to vote. You would smash it no doubt," says Philip.

"Blap, blap, blap," salute the crew.

I feel good yet I still can't look Nadine in the eyes. I look past her and as I walk towards the door Celestine says.

"Hi Leon! You were wicked. I hope that was about me."

I stop in my tracks and laugh.

"Yeah, course B, who else would it be about?" I answer with confidence and she giggles like crazy. She leans in and touches my arm.

"You so crazy Lee," she laughs.

"Just for you," I flirt, looking back at Nadine.

"Is it really?" Celestine continues with a flirtatious chuckle. I look her up and down, the way the big mans look the girls up and down. Like they want to eat them up there and then.

"Yeah... really... What you saying?" I ask.

Nadine releases a loud huff and barges past me. Rianna looks at me with raised eyebrows and Celestine moves in closer to me. I don't fancy Celestine but it's the only way I know how to deal with the Nadine situation. I don't want Nadine thinking that I'm all torn up about her. I don't want her to make a fool out of me so best to just let her see that she's not all that.

"Here's my number yeah."

She grabs my phone from my hand, taps her number into it before placing the phone back in my palm. Dad was right. I am fine.

I walk up the stairs to the top floor. Rianna and

Nadine are playing table tennis. As I walk past them. Nadine throws me a ghetto glare. She cuts her eyes at me hard and I laugh in response. Immature. I know.

She slams her bat down on the table and stomps off.

"What's wrong with you?" Rianna asks as she barges past me and runs after Nadine. Why are girls so funny? The girl said 'no'. I'm moving on and she's getting angry with me.

"Rianna!" I yell after her.

"What?" she answers.

"What do you mean what's wrong with me? What have I done?"

"Ehh, you ask Nadine out yesterday then all of a sudden you're all up on Celeste," she says, kissing her teeth.

"Yeah and Nadine said no init" I answer whilst using my hands to gesture my frustration.

"Yeah, but Celeste, Leon, Celeste!"

"What about Celestine?"

"Do you know why she said no Leon? Do you?" she asks, poking me in the chest with her index finger.

"Umm," I say rubbing my chin, "'cause she don't like me? 'Cause I'm not one of the big mans."

Rianna kisses her teeth again.

"No dummy. She's not allowed to have a boyfriend. If her dad catches her, he'll stop her coming out. That's why fool!"

"Seen," I answer, feeling pretty stupid.

"And one more thing yeah Leon. You don't go chatting up friends. You can't go from one friend to the other. That's just wrong." She stomps off leaving me feeling like an immature fool.

CHAPTER 15

"DOES THAT mean she likes me?" I ask Robert after telling him about my discussion with Rianna.

"Yeah probably. Ask her init," he answers.

"What? So she can blank me and say no again?" I say, shaking my head.

"Messenger her man."

"Eh... you have brains after all my man," I laugh as I quickly turn on my laptop and log-on to my messenger to find that she is online.

"What should I say?" I ask him as though he is the all-knower.

"Yo Leon, you're the lyrical mastermind," we both laugh.

"Tell her this. Just send her a message saying 'hey, how you doing'. If she answers, just chat with her init then ask her."

"Cool," I answer as I quickly type my message to her.

Within seconds Nadine replies.

Nadine: *Hi, I'm ql. U?*

Me: *I'm ight. Wat u up 2?*

Nadine: *Jst surfn. U nt wid ur yat?*

Me: *Who dat?*

Nadine: *Celestine.*

Me: *Lmao. She's nt my gal.*

Nadine: *Sure lokd lk it 2day.*

Me: *Wel she ain't. We were jst playn.*

Nadine: *Dz she no dat?*

Me: Yeah. I ain't called her or nuffink. Y all da questions. U jealous?

Nadine: *KMT*

Me: *U r init?*

Nadine: *y wd I b jealous?*

Me: *Cause u lk me?*

Nadine: *Whatever!*

Me: *So u dnt lk me?*

Nadine: *I never said dat.*

Me: *So do u?*

Nadine: *I never said dat!*

Me: *So wat u sayn?*

Nadine: *Nuffink. I ain't sayn nuffink.*

Me: *Is it true you said no cause of ur dad?*

Nadine: *Who told you dat?*

Me: *Is it?*

Nadine: *Might be.*

Me: *So u do lk me?*

Nadine: *What diff ds it make?*

Me: *Send me 2 smiley faces if it is a yes.*

Nadine: :-) :-). *Lol*

I feel so happy and excited. Nadine Simmonds likes me. Rah! I'm a bad man. I'm Leman, the foiinee boy.

Me: *So if your dad wasn't strict, wd u go out wid me?*

Nadine: *Don't go gettn a big head. Yeah I wd. Ur QL. Y were u chattn Celeste up?*

Me: *To make u jealous.*

Nadine: *Fool!*

Me: *Were U?*

Nadine: *Wat?*

Me: *You knw wat.*

"Yo! Lover boy. I'm out," Robert says behind me, but I'm too busy typing excitedly to Nadine. To busy making her LOL and LMAO. Too busy keeping her online.

Me: *B my cyber gal.. .think bout it.. .tell me 2morrow.*

I log off before she has a chance to respond. I'm a lyrical mastermind. A smooth brother. I'm dapper and I know it, now, she knows it too.

CHAPTER 16

"TONIGHT'S THE big night bruv," Mensah says jumping up and down like some crazed kangaroo.

"What night?" I ask, uninterested. I know what night it is but I'm still in a sulk because I don't have a part to play.

"The spit on the mic competition init, down at North Westminster."

"Seen."

"You on it?"

"Yeah man. I'm there. Yo, what's the prize?"

"You ready for it?" he asks.

"Go on man!"

"Open two shows yeah. N-dubz at Shepherd's Bush, Dizzie Rascal's at Brixton and then... are you ready to hear this bruv?"

"Talk nah man!" I snap as the feeling of jealousy multiplies within me.

"We get to meet Kanye West at his next show. Can you imagine that bruv?"

"NO!" I scream like a big girl.

"Yes mate, check mate, bet you wish it was you mate, but your late mate, bruv don't hate," Mensah chats, bopping his head like he is on stage.

"That's wiggidy wiggidy wack mate," I laugh wondering to myself if they really have a chance of winning with lyrics like those.

"Come practice with us in studio man," Mensah says as he begins walking down the stairs. I follow him and half-way down the stairs I notice Nadine walking up the steps.

"I'll catch you in a minute yeah?" I yell out to Mensah as I stop in front of Nadine. She smiles and cocks her head to the side.

"You alright?" I ask confidently with my chin up in her direction.

"Yeah. You?" she smiles, batting her eyelashes.

"What you doing?" I ask.

"Waiting for the girls. Practice and that."

"Seen. So...What you saying?" I smile staring her straight in the eye. I can't believe I'm chatting like this to Nadine Simmonds. Chatting with a lean and a swagger, an air of confidence and a touch of arrogance.

"'Bout what?" She asks staring right back at me

with her girly smile. Her white teeth exposed like a Colgate advert.

"If I can't have you in reality, will you be my gal in our digital galaxy? Log into you secretly, I'll be your firewall baby with maximum security," I chat, bobbing and moving closer towards her. My heart races with excitement as I grab her hands and swing them around. Alone in the stairway, I'm up close to her; my nose almost touching hers.

"Will you be my cyber queen?" I finally whisper as I lean in to kiss her. She kisses me back, tongues softly mingling whilst our heads angle us in the perfect position. The warmth of her tongue excites me and I just want to keep her there, but we hear footsteps and we pull apart. I let her hands go and she giggles.

Amelia and Vanilla walk past us; she turns her back to me and begins walking up the stairs.

"Yo Nadine!" I yell behind her. She turns around and her ponytail swishes from left to right. She smiles her full teeth smile and leans her head at an angle. She is so pretty.

"I take it that is a yes then?" I ask smiling, feeling like a don. She pouts her small pink lips and simply nods.

Nadine Simmonds is my cyber girl. This is the best day of my life.

CHAPTER 17

I COORDINATE my outfit carefully for tonight. Baggy jeans with my white Armani diamond mic t-shirt. I brush my low-cut hair and admire myself in the mirror.

"Leeeon, you foinne boy!" I laugh to myself.

"Lord have mercy. You done gone and lost your mind. You joker about Leeeeeeeeeeeeeon, you fooooinne boy!" My sister laughs with her head in the door.

"You never heard of knocking Latti? I could have been naked!" I yell.

"Please, I used to bath you. Hehe hehe hehe, you too funny. Anyway Dark Vader, when you leaving?"

"Ten minutes pinky."

"Seen, will you wait for me?" she asks.

"Ten minutes sis. Ten minutes GMT time not BMT yeah?"

"Yessir," she answers as she shuts my door.

My MSN Messenger flashes orange. I do a quick mirror check before I answer and turn on my webcam.

"Yo!" I answer.

"Hey, you alright?"

"Yeah man, what's going down?" I ask.

"What time you reaching the Spit?" she says as she puts her big gold hoops through her ears.

"Leaving in ten minutes with my sister."

"Alright. I'll see you there."

"Laters B."

The school hall has been well organised. A huge stage is in front of the large room and barriers set out in front of the stage like a real concert. Graffiti posters of red music notes and rappers' silhouettes are plastered on the wall behind the stage, whilst the other walls in the hall have rappers names written in bold. The hip hop beat is booming through the enormous speakers and it is creating a lively atmosphere. The school hall fills up quickly with excited teenagers, chatting and screeching like mad. The organisers dim down the lights making the whole event feel like a real rave. Tonight is going to be wicked!

From the corner of my eye, I notice Robert with

Rianna and Nadine. They walk up to me and Robert and I slap our hands together and jump up and down excitedly.

I look down at Nadine who looks real cute, decked out in her pink skinny jeans and pick v-neck top. Her hair is out, bouncing around her face whilst her lips are shiny. I grab my girl's hand and she squeezes mine.

In the front row, we stand awaiting the start of the big night when suddenly the music changes and dancers somersault onto the stage. The crowd goes wild, people whistle, others clap, whilst the girls scream. The dance group go wild in their army uniform, body popping, head spinning and moving in sync. The routine is sick and Rianna is engrossed. She stands there with her jaw wide open and eyes fixated on the stage. As the routine comes to an end, the crowd goes wild, stamping their feet, clapping their hands and saluting them with the legendary 'blap blap'. The atmosphere is off the chain: it's crazy and I can't get this wild smile off my face.

The compere comes on full of energy, bouncing up and down. His voice is loud, his mood is high and his words cause the crowd to go mental again.

"People are you rea..aa..dy?" he sings.

"NO!" the crowd responds.

"Were they bad or were they bad?" he asks, shaking his head. The crowd go wild with hysteria.

"Boys and girls, are you ready for a big night? Are you ready for a crazy night? Full of rhythm and talent?"

'Yes!" the crowd screams.

"I can't hear you," he continues.

"I said, people, are you ready for a crazy night?"

We all respond an even louder yes.

"That's what I'm saying, that's more like it. Boys and girls, welcome to talentville, home to raw, fresh talent where a minute of talent is uploaded every minute. Log-on! Vote! And if you have talent, upload it! You never know who is watching, you never know who is signing. Tonight we have mans from East London, mans from West London, South London and North London. Now tell me, where you representing? If you from south let me hear ya."

The presenter continues to hype the crowd up and I'm mad excited. For a moment, my envy disappears.

He finally introduces the first group as the 'Swagger Crew' from North London.

All six boys come onto stage co-ordinated in all white. The look the part as they swagger onto the stage with attitude.

The DJ drops the beat and one after the other they begin to chat. Their well-rehearsed routine is wicked.

They've even choreographed some dance into their routine and the crowd loves them. As their four minutes roll to an end the crowd roars with appreciation. The compare comes back out still bouncing like he's drunk too much Coke.

"Well done boys," he says enthusiastically.

"I'm loving the coordination and routine. Anyways it's the heat mic time," he tells them, smiling like a Cheshire cat. "You have two minutes to chat about road block to this beat."

A tall, dark-skinned boy comes forward. He doesn't smile; he just takes the mic and rhymes to the beat without any hesitation. He smacks it with confidence and composure and again it sends the crowd bonkers. The judges score them 35 out of 40. The judges praise the solo MC and, in a way, I'm glad that I'm not part of the crew because the competition is tight.

CHAPTER 18

THE SECOND group come on, they are all girls and they call themselves 'Da Honeyz'. They drop their lyrics and captivate the audience with their words and seductive body movements. The crowd go wild, especially the boys. The girls are good, but I know Amelia is much better than that. She flows better, she rhymes harder and she has something different about her voice.

"Your topic is broken pencil," says the presenter and without time to digest the topic, the beat drops. The short Moroccan-looking girl starts well, but messes up her lines as she goes on. The judges scores them 29.

The third group are called 'Toy Soldiers' and their beat is hypnotizing. I'm busy bobbing my head and rhyming in mind when I feel someone yank my arm aggressively. My natural instinct is to turn around and shove the perpetrator but as I turn I notice Skull Head and Vanilla looking stressed.

"Yo!Yo!" is all I can hear.

"What?" I yell as they drag me away from the front row through to the back. I move my feet reluctantly as I want to see Toy Soldiers' performance because, by the sound of it, they are doing some serious damage to the mic.

"Yo, Mensah's done messed us up man!" Skull Head says, punching into the air.

"What happened?" I ask.

"Fool ate some biscuits with nuts init and he had some serious allergy attack. I swear that brother is dizzie blod."

"No! Don't lie," I gasp.

"No lie. We're on after them lot on stage and we need a body so you are on."

"WHAT!" I scream like a woman in shock.

"No time man. You need to replace Mensah," Vanilla says, walking off towards backstage.

The room freezes. The hands of the clock stand still and my alter ego pops up on my right shoulder whilst fear sits dangling its feet on my left shoulder.

Fear says, "Leon, don't do it. Imagine messing up

HERE! In front of all these people. Nah mate."

"Shut up scaredy cat," says my alter ego.

"Yo blod. You're a bad man and you know it. A lyrical mastermind. You've spent all that time practicing. Don't waste the opportunity. Take it. Grab it by the horns and do your thing. You can do it. You can do anything you want to do today, tomorrow, always; just believe in yourself."

I feel like some Walt Disney character with thc clichés spinning in my mind. The clock ticks, the noise returns and all is unfrozen again.

"I'm on it," I reply as I bounce backstage to meet the crew.

We quickly practice while the Toy Soldiers perform,

"If the topic is about fights, I'm on it," says Skull Head.

"If it's about fashion, it's mine," replies Amelia.

"If it's about school or food, mine!" inputs Vanilla.

I stand there uncoordinated, unlike the rest of them in all black hooded Adidas tracksuits. I wonder to myself what topic I can claim, but my mind is blank.

"You're on. Mash it up!" Philip yells out of the blue and I swear my heart is about to jump out of my chest.

My heart races at hundred miles an hour. The blood pumps vigorously whilst the beating violently bounces up against my ribcage. I feel like my chest is about to explode.

Sweat gathers around my forehead and my palms become super clammy. The crew bounce up and down to shake away the nervousness and hype themselves up.

"Yo group hug," says Vanilla and, to my surprise, everyone gathers together and we hug. The tension is strong and the nervousness is rife as we let go of each other.

We run onto the stage and, like my dream, I see the crowd ahead of me, screaming, bouncing and going wild. Unlike the Swagger Crew we don't have a dance routine nor are we all pretty and hot like Da Honeyz, but boy we have talent. I know it, we know it and now everyone listening is going to know it.

Skull Head starts off and the crowd is mesmerised. The girls are all goggle-eyed as he serenades them with his sweet church boy voice. Amelia takes over and blows it apart with her faultless flow and the crowd go mental with their 'blapping' salutes. The salutes are echoed when Vanilla shows them what he's made of. It feels wicked hearing Da Crew perform and hearing the crowd respond in such a crazy way. I'm hyped, I'm ready, I'm gagging for it as I morph from Leon, the 15-year-old schoolboy, into Leman, the Lyrical Mastermind.

With a mic in my hand, I keep it flowing, I keep the crowd going. I'm bouncing, I'm laughing, and I can't believe they are sapping it all up. I chat with my hands, my feet, all I have inside of me and when my time is up, I'm on a high.

The noise is immense. The feedback is amazing. I'm so hyped, I don't want to get off the stage.

"Right guys. That was wicked. Now your topic is cyber love."

All their faces drop, but I smile. I know all about cyber love and, even better, I'm lyrically prepared for it.

CHAPTER 19

I GRIP the mic for dear life and suddenly the words escape me. I'm speechless, I'm lyricless and the beat starts pumping through the giant black speakers.

I look into the crowd and I see my sister smiling and nodding her head. I see Robert clapping excitedly and Nadine jumping. I have to do this. I have to rip up the mic. Jigger man did it, Dizzie did it and so will I.

I open my mouth and, without control, the words flow out smooth and sleek. I chat about my newfound 'cyber gal'. I use the words from the digital world. Megabytes, webcam, wireless, dial-up and I mix them up with thoughts of girls. I rip up the mic like no other and the crowd loves it. They stamp their feet hard on the ground and they holler and hoot. The rest of the crew pat me on the back as the music suddenly comes to a halt. The adrenaline is still high inside me as the sweat beads roll down my face.

CHAPTER 20

"YOUNG MAN, you have some real talent, keep on practising and you'll go far," says the first wide-eyed judge.

"I'm going to give you a 10," he continues.

We all go crazy up on stage, jumping like crazy while a section of the crowd stamps and roars in agreement.

"As a group," says the second judge, "you are quality. A mish mash of great talent. That's a 10 from me."

I can't believe it. I can't believe that despite our lack of perfect coordination and dance moves in our routine we are still scoring highly.

"Real quality. I totally enjoyed that performance. I just wish you had put a little something else in. Maybe some moves or just something visual, you get what I'm saying?"

The smiles on our faces drop. We know this judge isn't going to give us ten points.

"7," he finally says and a section of the crowd let out a loud booing sound.

The excitement suddenly disappears and I smell the fear as we all breathe heavily. This final judge could make us or break us. If she scores us any less than eight points then we've lost and the Swagger Crew has won.

"We'll, I thought you were good, but with time you will get better. Focus during poetry when you are in school and you'll hit the top."

We are all breathing heavily, clinging on tight to each other's arms. Anticipation is high up in the air and we just need to see the score. I take a deep breath in as she finally turns her card over.

"9," she yells with a great big smile across her face.

I scream like my mother and turn to the rest of the crew who are going mad with excitement.

"Well done guys. You have won the big prize and your night as stars starts tonight. Ladies and gentlemen, give it up for talentville's latest winners… Da Crew.'

"Da Crew! Da Crew! Da Crew!" The crowd chant as I shake my head and bounce from my knees. I feel the lyrics bubbling up in my stomach, rising slowly through my veins, like the hulk I'm morphing once again from Leon to Leman: the master of the mic, the man whose skills bring out the chills. I can feel the notes moving in my blood, through my heart and out of my lungs. As I open up my mouth to spit on the mic, the crowd goes crazy. Nadine Simmonds screams.

Got Talent? Raw, Fresh Talent?
ONE MINUTE
Talent
Ville
co.uk

The Lisson Green Chronicles

ROBERT-SLAM!

All Robert wants to do is play ball. He is fifteen, 5' 6" and the best player on the team. He knows he has potential to go far but his strict Nigerian mother isn't hearing it. "Doctor, lawyer, accountant..." is all she says. How does Robert fulfil his dream and keep his mother happy at the same time?

Buy a copy at www.urbantopia.co.uk

Coming soon to Urbantopia Books

The Lisson Green Chronicles

Rianna – Tearful Dancer

Rianna's biggest dream is to be a dancer. She has rhythm, she is coordinated, and she has talent, but she is also the child of a physically abusive man.

When faced with the opportunity to go away to a dance school in America, Rianna is torn between achieving her dream and leaving her younger sisters behind unprotected. She must decide on what is more important.